The Goosehill Gang

and the
Shadow on the Shade

by Mary Blount Christian
illustrated by Betty Wind

Contribute to the needs of the saints, practice hospitality.
Romans 12:13 RSV

Publishing House
St. Louis

In memory of G. L. Christian, who lived Romans 12:13

Concordia Publishing House, St. Louis, Missouri
Copyright © 1978 Concordia Publishing House
Manufactured in the United States of America

Library of Congress Cataloging in Publication Data

Christian, Mary Blount.
    The Goosehill Gang and the shadow on the shade.

    SUMMARY: The Goosehill Gang helps find a job for a recently paroled convict.
    [1. Ex-convicts—Fiction. 2. Parole—Fiction]
I. Wind, Betty.   II. Title.
PZ7.C4528Gpo   [Fic]   78-1291
ISBN 0-570-07358-8

"I can't play!" Marcus snapped. He closed the
door with a quick click. Don stood on the Moreno's
front porch staring at the door that had been closed
in his face. He turned on his heels and stomped
down the steps. He was so angry he could feel his
cheeks burning.

Don pedaled to Tubby's. "Boy!" he told his
friend. "I don't get it! Marcus is as snappish as an old
crocodile."

Tubby settled on the step next to Don. "You should have seen him in school today if you think that's bad. He was nasty to everybody, and he didn't even turn in that English assignment and wouldn't tell Mrs. Pruitt why."

"Marcus?" Don asked. "I've never known him to skip homework. That's not like him."

Tubby grinned. "Yeah, you maybe, but not Marcus!"

Beth slid her bike to a quick stop. She stood it next to Don's and dropped to the step next to the

4

boys. "Ooooh, I'm so mad!" she stormed. "That Marcus is so mean! He . . . he practically threw me off his porch!"

"Maybe he doesn't want to be our friend any more," Tubby said. "Maybe he doesn't want to be a member of the Goosehill Gang either."

Don took off his baseball cap. He slapped it against his knee. "Yeah? Well, maybe we can fix that! Maybe we ought to drop him from the club."

Beth sighed. "I think we need to do something. But what?"

"Maybe Pete will have an idea," Tubby said. "Why don't we have a meeting this afternoon and take a vote?"

"Pete has a piano lesson this afternoon," Beth said. "We'll have to have a meeting at the tree house tomorrow right after school."

The children agreed. "Don't you think we should ask Marcus to come?" Tubby said. "After all, it's kind of sneaky to vote without giving him a chance to tell us his side."

Beth called Pete that evening and told him about the meeting. "I'm in the same classroom with Marcus," Pete said. "I'll tell him about the meeting tomorrow. I wouldn't feel right calling him on the phone. He should hear it face to face."

At school the next morning Pete saw Marcus start into the classroom. He ran after him, but nearly ran into him when Marcus stopped studdenly. He was staring at the black board. Some of the children whispered and giggled as Marcus, hunched over his books, slid into his desk without looking up again.

Pete stared at the blackboard. His mouth opened in surprise. It read, "MARCUS MORENO IS A JAILBIRD." And under the scribbled letters there was a picture of a bird in striped clothes.

Mrs. Pruitt walked into her classroom. Without a word and without looking at any of the children, she erased the board. The whispers stopped when she turned to face the class. Pete turned to look at Marcus. He hadn't moved. He was still holding his schoolbooks tightly and staring down at his desk.

Mrs. Pruit began the lessons without saying anything about the blackboard. The class was quiet. Some of the children would glance at Marcus quickly, then look away. At lunch Pete caught up to him. "What was that all about, Marcus? Why would anybody write that about you? And what is a jailbird?"

"Look it up if you want to know," Marcus said without looking at Pete. "And besides my name is Marcus Moreno Junior!"

Marcus started to walk away, but Pete put his hand on his shoulder to stop him. "There's a meeting of the Goosehill Gang after school. Come to the tree house. It's about you."

Pushing his glasses back on his nose, Marcus asked, "What about me?"

Pete shrugged. "Well, you have to admit that you're acting kind of unfriendly. We need to work things out or . . ."

"Or what?" Marcus interrupted.

"Or," Pete continued, "stop being friends and maybe drop you from the Goosehill Gang."

Marcus' face grew apple red. Lines formed on his forehead. "Maybe we've already stopped being friends! And as for the gang, do what you want to. I don't care." He stalked off, leaving Pete staring after him.

Pete recalled the scene to the other members in the tree house after school "Well, I never!" Beth yelled. "The nerve of that Marcus!"

Tubby slammed his fist into his other palm. "I say we drop him! Right now!"

Don spoke up. "I looked in my bird book. There's no such thing as a jailbird. So I don't know what that note meant."

Beth said, "You were looking in the wrong book. I looked in the dictionary. A jailbird is someone who has spent time in jail."

"That's stupid!" Tubby said. "Marcus has never been in jail!"

"I think we should find out the reason Marcus is acting so weird. I think we should keep a close watch on him," Don said.

"You mean spy!" Beth said.

Don shrugged. "I'd like to think of it as looking out for a friend." He pulled a long tube from behind the crate that was their tree house table. "And I have made just the thing for looking."

The children gathered closer. "This is a periscope," Don explained. "It's kind of like the ones they use on submarines. You know, they can be underwater and look on top of the water with one."

The children took turns looking through the periscope. "It really works!" Beth said. "How'd you do that?"

Don grinned. "With a cardboard mailing tube and mirrors. It was easy. I figure we can hide behind the hedge and take turns watching the house with this."

Tubby shook his head. "It's no use. I went by there on the way here. All the shades were closed."

"Well, maybe that's because Marcus is expecting us during the day," Don said. "If we can stay out a little after dark, maybe he won't expect us."

Tubby jumped up. "If I'm going to do any night watching I'd better get home and do my homework right now."

"Me too!" Beth said. The children agreed to meet outside Marcus' hedge after supper.

The boys were already squatting behind the hedge when Beth got there. "The shades are still down," Tubby whispered.

"Yeah," Beth said. "But somebody just turned on the light."

Don looked through the periscope. "I see Marcus' shadow on the shade. See? You can see the shape of his glasses and the way his hair kind of goes

in all directions." He passed the periscope around. The children each looked.

"There's Mrs. Moreno!" Beth said. "I can see the shadow of her wheelchair."

Again the children took turns. When it was Don's turn again he gasped, "Oh, no ."

The children crept close and eagerly stared through the periscope. "There's a third shadow in the room," Tubby said. "And it's a big one."

Don nodded. "It's definitely not the shadow of another kid. Look at how much bigger it is than Marcus." Beth's eyes widened. "It's a man's shadow. Do . . . you think that Marcus and his mother are . . . prisoners?"

"You mean like hostages?" Pete asked, scratching his chin thoughtfully. "Prisoners, ummm. That would maybe explain the note on the blackboard. Jailbird, prisoner. But who'd write that on the board? Who is in that class that could know?"

Tubby snapped his fingers. "Marcus would know! Maybe he was trying to get a message to us."

"Naw," Pete argued. "Why wouldn't he just tell us? Besides, he was at school. That doesn't sound much like a prisoner to me."

Beth twirled one of her pigtails as she mulled it over. "But Mrs. Moreno doesn't go to school. Maybe Marcus is afraid because she is at home with the shadow. Maybe he can't say anything."

"Beth could be right," Pete said. "Maybe we should call the police."

"And tell them what?" Don said. "That we saw a strange shadow on the shade? That one of our friends acts weird?"

Pete sank back. "You're right. We need proof. We'll just have to wait a while longer."

"But what about Marcus and Mrs. Moreno?" Beth pleaded. "We can't leave them in there with the shadow!"

Don spoke. "We know they are all right. But if we break in there like the cavalry they might not be.

14

We'll watch. And we'll get our chance. I don't think the shadow is going to hurt them. He hasn't so far."

The children agreed. They went to their homes. When Don got home his father was bent over the desk with wadded papers scattered in and around the waste basket. "Don't tell me you have homework too!" Don teased. He was glad for a lighter moment.

Mr. Richards stuck the pencil behind his ear and leaned back to stretch. "I'm trying to finish figuring all the business expenses, but I'm just not good at bookkeeping. My trouble is I'm too small a business to hire a full-time bookkeeper. But I'm too big now to do it myself. It's an awkward stage for a business."

"I guess we kids understand that problem," Don said. "We are always too big for this and too little for that too." Mr. Richards laughed and gave his son a friendly pat on the shoulder.

"Why don't we raid the cookie jar, then play a game of scrabble? It has to be easier than those books." The two of them agreed.

On the way to school the next morning Don decided to stop by Marcus' house. He parked his bike and walked around to the back. If Marcus was still there he'd probably be eating breakfast. And maybe the shadow wouldn't expect anyone at the back door. Maybe Marcus could talk without being seen.

Don had almost turned the corner of the house when he spotted a man sitting on the back steps. He was slumped over with his heads in his hands. Don stared at him. Could this be the shadow? He didn't look very scary to Don. In fact he looked to Don more like he needed help.

Don swallowed hard, then bounded up. "Hi!" he said. The man sat straight up, startled. He blinked at Don. But he didn't say anything.

"I'm Don Richards."

Awkwardly the man stuck out his hand. "I'm . . . I'm Marcus Moreno."

Don stared at the man. "Marcus? You . . . you mean you are kin to Marcus? Are you an uncle?"

The man shook his head. "No. I'm Marcus senior. He is my son."

Don could feel his chin sag. He stared open mouthed for a second before answering. "But . . . but you're his father? I, that is, we all thought you were dead!"

"I am, Don. I guess I am," Mr. Moreno said sadly. He nodded a good-bye to Don, then went inside.

Don stared toward the closed door trying to understand. But suddenly he remembered it was a school day. Quickly he pedaled to school. He was almost late and didn't get to tell the other children what he'd learned. Don fidgeted all during class until the lunchbell rang. Then he shot out the door and down the hall to the rest of the Goosehill Gang.

He motioned them to follow. They found Marcus leaning against the building outside. "Marcus," Don began. "Why did you tell us your father was dead?" Beth, Pete and Tubby looked from one to the other, but none of them spoke.

Marcus' face tightened. "I never said that! You did!"

Don crossed his arms over his chest and glared back. "Yeah? Well, you never corrected us. Why didn't you tell us your father was alive?"

Beth stepped closer. "Marcus! I . . . I thought we were your friends! Why would you keep such a secret from us?"

Tubby shook his head. "Yeah, Marcus. You never told us he was alive. And you never told us he was here!"

Marcus stared at the ground. His eyes looked

moist behind his glasses. "I . . . I didn't tell you because you probably wouldn't want to be my friend if you knew. My . . . my father was in prison. He just got out."

"Prison!" Beth gasped. "But why?"

Marcus looked at them grimly. "It's none of your business. Just leave me alone." He stomped off, leaving the gang to stare after him.

"Wow!" Beth said. "The shadow on the shade was his father!" The gang talked among themselves. They agreed to meet after school and to visit the Morenos.

Mrs. Moreno met them at the door. "Come in," she said, smiling. "I've been expecting you." They pushed her wheelchair into the kitchen where Mr. Moreno nodded as his wife called out their names. He pulled out some cups and poured hot chocolate for them.

Beth looked around. "Where's Marcus?"

"In his room," Mrs. Moreno replied. "He heard you come in I think. But he isn't quite ready to see you."

"You're his friends," Mr. Moreno said. "So I want you to know I was in prison. When I went in,

Marcus and Janet moved here to Goosehill. They left Springer where everybody knew. Marcus needed a new school so he wouldn't be ashamed."

"Ashamed?" Beth interrupted. But Mr. Moreno raised his hand to silence her. "Please, just let me finish. I was a bookkeeper. I made a good salary. But we needed lots more. Janet needed operations. I took the money from the company I worked for. I was caught and sent to prison."

"But why?" Don asked. "Couldn't you get it some other way?"

Mr. Moreno shrugged. "Yes, as it turned out. I forgot a very important thing, or maybe I just never knew. I never realized that there are lots of people like you kids who are willing to help. The people in Springer Creek—people we didn't even know— donated money to help. They even raised money with bake sales to help pay the hospital bills of a stranger. And some of the doctors donated their time, too."

Mrs. Moreno smiled at her husband. "We were able to give most of the money back to the company. And we hope to pay back the rest, too."

Mr. Moreno patted his wife's hand. "And Janet is getting stronger every day. She'll be walking again soon."

Tubby sipped the last of his chocolate. "Then everything is going to be all right now, huh? I mean

you're back home and Mrs. Moreno's going to be okay."

"I'm afraid it isn't that easy, Tubby," Mr. Moreno said with a sigh. I can't get a job here. I've tried, but there aren't too many openings for full-time bookkeepers in Goosehill, especially if you've been in prison."

"You mean you might move?" Beth asked. "You and your family might leave Goosehill?"

Mr. Moreno shrugged. "Not my family. Maybe just me. I mean it would be hard on them. And Marcus is so unhappy."

Don spoke up. "Mr. Moreno, you forgot once that people can help. Please don't forget it this time. Maybe we can think of something."

"Yes," Beth added. "You've shown Marcus that you love your family enough to do something wrong. Now show him you love them enough to do something right!"

Mr. Moreno stared at her. "Meaning?" he asked.

"Meaning that you stay here where they're happy and that you don't turn down the help of friends," Beth said. Don suddenly leaped from his chair. "What an idea! See you later!" he called over his shoulder as he burst through the door.

Don pedaled home as fast as he could. He bounded through the door and shouted, "Dad! I've got a terrific surprise for you!" Quickly he told Mr. Richards about Marcus' father. "So you see," he continued. "You wouldn't have to work extra hours on your books. And he'd have a job. It's perfect!"

But Mr. Richards shook his head. "It wouldn't work out. I can't afford to pay him enough money since I still don't have that much work. "And," Mr. Richards said, "He did go to prison for stealing, remember."

Don stared at his father. "I . . . I can understand about the small pay. But Dad! You've got to give him a chance. The Morenos might move, or worse, Mr. Moreno might go alone! You can't let that happen. You just can't!"

"I'll think about it. But there's still the problem of too little pay," Mr. Richards reminded his son.

Don leaned forward. "Goosehill is growing. There are other businesses like yours. There must be

at least two more that could use somebody part time. Put them together and it's like a full-time job!"

Mr. Richards nodded thoughtfully. "Maybe. But who will be willing to trust him?"

Don clutched his baseball cap tightly. "Why not start with your men's group at church, Dad? After all, isn't that what it's all about? I mean forgiving?"

Mr. Richards patted Don on the shoulder. "Did I ever tell you I not only love you, but I like you very much?"

Don sat eagerly by his father as Mr. Richards made a half dozen phone calls to friends. When he was finished, he had two other businesses that would give Mr. Moreno jobs.

"They'll be temporary," Mr. Richards told Don. "He'll be almost on trial again."

"He'll do great! I know he will," Don assured him.

The next week Don and the rest of the gang stopped to see Marcus. Mr. Moreno answered the door. "I . . . thought you were working!" Don said.

"I am! I pick up the books and work on them here. It gives me a chance to get reacquainted with my wife and son," he explained.

Marcus came in. He placed his hand on his father's shoulder. "He's really good at math. He's even better than you are, Tubby!"

"I bet I can beat him at one thing," Tubby boasted.

"Oh? What's that?" Mr. Moreno asked. "Addition?"

"Eating!" the members of the Goosehill Gang shouted at once. "Eating!"

And they all went into the Moreno's kitchen to prove it.